Bacon Cheese Murder

Book Two

in

Papa Pacelli's

Pizzeria Series

By

Patti Benning

ISBN:9781539030218

**This book is a work of fiction. Any similarities to persons, living or dead, places of business, or situations past or present, is completely unintentional.

Author's Note: On the next page, you'll find out how to access all of my books easily, as well as locate books by best-selling author, Summer Prescott. I'd love to hear your thoughts on my books, the storylines, and anything else that you'd like to comment on – reader feedback is very important to me. Please see the following page for my publisher's contact information. If you'd like to be on her list of "folks to contact" with updates, release and sales notifications, etc…just shoot her an email and let her know. Thanks for reading!

Also…

…if you're looking for more great reads, from me and Summer, check out the Summer Prescott Publishing Book Catalog:

http://summerprescottbooks.com/book-catalog/ for some truly delicious stories.

Contact Info for Summer Prescott Publishing:

Twitter: @summerprescott1

Blog and Book Catalog: http://summerprescottbooks.com

Email: summer.prescott.cozies@gmail.com

And…look up The Summer Prescott Fan Page on Facebook – let's be friends!

If you're an author and are interested in publishing with Summer Prescott Books – please send Summer an email and she'll send you submission guidelines.

TABLE OF CONTENTS

BACON CHEESE
MURDER

Book Two in Papa Pacelli's Pizzeria Series

CHAPTER ONE

Eleanora Pacelli pulled open the oven and peered inside. What she saw made her smile.

"Perfect," she said, reaching for the oven mitt. "Nonna, come sit down… it's done."

She took the pizza stone out of the oven and placed it on a rack, then pulled the pizza wheel out of a drawer. Expertly, precisely, she sliced the pizza into eighths, then transferred the entire stone to a trivet on the small table in the breakfast nook. Her grandmother Ann Pacelli had already taken her seat. The old woman, with her professionally curled white hair and turquoise reading glasses, eyed the pizza critically for a moment, then beamed.

"It looks just like how your grandfather used to make it," she said. "This was always one of my favorite dinners. Sausage and tomato pizza with real mozzarella… it was the first pizza he ever made for me."

Ellie smiled, glad that she had been able to bring back good memories for the elderly woman who had done so much for her over the past few weeks. It was a good start on the long road to making up for all of the years she had neglected to visit after moving away as a teen. Twenty-five years was a long time to go without seeing someone, though, and it would take a lot more than a pizza dinner to alleviate some of the guilt she felt about it.

“Don’t compliment me just yet,” Ellie said, reaching for a piece. “Let’s see how it tastes first.”

The pizza was just about perfect. The cheese was melted and gooey, the sauce was bursting with flavor, and the crust was light and airy. In the weeks since Ellie had moved back to Kittiport, Maine, she had had a crash course on pizza making. Taking over her grandfather’s pizzeria, Papa Pacelli’s, hadn’t been easy, but it had been rewarding—more so than any job she’d ever had. She took pride in creating something with her own hands, even if that something was only a pizza.

They ate their lunch in a comfortable silence. Bunny, Ellie’s little black-and-white papillon, waited eagerly under the table for dropped tidbits. Ellie had the suspicion that her grandmother was sneaking the dog little bits of sausage, but couldn't complain—she was saving her last pizza crust for Marlowe, after all.

The large parrot was hanging on the cage bars when Ellie left the kitchen after finishing lunch with her grandmother. She greeted Ellie with a loud squawk, and the woman smiled. Marlowe, a green-winged macaw, had been her grandfather's. The bird had been devastated after he passed away, and was just now beginning to show her normal, undepressed, personality. Ellie had never had a bird, and was still wary of that big, bone-colored beak, but was quickly learning just how much personality the parrot had. She was a joy to interact with.

"I've got a treat for you, Marlowe," she said as she opened the cage door. "Pizza." She held up the pizza crust, watching the bird's light gold pupils shrink to pinpricks as she recognized one of her favorite foods.

With a smile, Ellie handed her the crust. The bird held it in one clawed foot, while nibbling small pieces off with her beak.

"What do you say?" she prodded gently. Her beak full of pizza crust, Marlowe gave a garbled "thank you," and Ellie smiled. The bird was smart, that was certain. She was nineteen years old, and had been raised since she was a chick by Arthur and Ann Pacelli. She was constantly surprising Ellie by saying something new, and often what she said was in context.

"Well, I've got to go to work," the woman said. "Goodbye."

She opened the front door, paused to scratch Bunny behind the ears, and smiled when she heard the bird call "Goodbye!" after a second. Between the bird and the dog, she knew her grandmother wouldn't be lonely.

Papa Pacelli's was in downtown Kittiport, not far from the marina. The old brick building had housed the pizzeria for nearly twenty years, making the restaurant a real fixture in town. It had lost popularity over the last two years as her grandfather stepped back from managing it. The young man that he had hired as manager turned out not to be as trustworthy as he hoped. Xavier Hurst had spent his two years there stealing funds from the pizzeria, and had done little to ensure that the other employees completed their tasks. With orders often getting delivered late and cold, and the pizzeria itself falling into disrepair, the restaurant ended up losing most of its customer base.

All that changed after Ellie took over. Once she found out that Xavier had been stealing from the pizzeria, she fired him and took over as manager herself. The other employees, Rose, Jacob, and Clara, had all done much better since she had made it clear that she wouldn't allow any more fooling around at work… especially if it kept the customers waiting.

She got to the restaurant shortly before Jacob and Rose were supposed to arrive. It was a good feeling to walk into a clean and organized kitchen. She opened one fridge and smiled to see neatly organized rows of balled pizza dough on the shelves. The top two shelves had Ellie's favorite thick-crust pizza dough, and on the bottom was their dough for thin-crust pizzas. Although Ellie had grown up in Kittiport, the decades she'd spent in Chicago had made her a true lover of thick-crust pizza. She considered the thin-crust pizza much preferred by easterners to be not much better than tomato sauce on crackers. The other fridge was stocked with all sorts of vegetables, cheeses, and meats, while the pantry held dry ingredients for various sauces, as well as the flour and yeast required to make the dough. Nearly everything they served was made from scratch, something that Ellie knew her grandfather had been very proud of.

We really do make the best pizza in town, she thought as she fired up the ovens. To be fair, there wasn't much competition… other than Cheesaroni Calzones. *I still can't believe that Jeffrey hired*

Xavier after I fired him. How can he trust him? It would serve him right if Xavier stole from him, too.

She wasn't usually a vengeful person, but the owner of the calzone shop had been nothing but rude to her ever since she arrived in town. She suspected that he and Xavier had been behind the sabotage that had taken place at the pizzeria a few weeks ago—in fact, she all but knew that they were behind it—but with no evidence against them, the best she had been able to do was to change the locks and keep an eye open for any more suspicious activity from the pair of them. She had the feeling that she hadn't heard the last of them yet.

"Hi Ms. Pacelli," one of the employees said as she came in through the back entrance. "How was your weekend?"

"Pretty good, Rose. Thanks for asking. How was yours?"

"Great." The young woman grinned. "I went down to Portland with some friends. We had pizza, but it was nowhere near as good as it is here."

"I'm glad to hear that," Ellie said, smiling. "Take a moment to clock in and get settled, then will you start folding some boxes? I'm going to go unlock the front doors. Fold a few more than you usually do. If this week is anything like last week, we'll need them."

CHAPTER TWO

It was a busy day, and Ellie couldn't have been happier. Her customers seemed happy too, and she was even beginning to recognize some local faces. *Soon enough I'll know the regulars by name*, she thought as she scrubbed her hands before leaving for the evening. *Hopefully they won't consider me an outsider for too much longer.* She had spent the first sixteen years of her life in Kittiport, after all. She had moved away in her junior year of high school after her parents got divorced. Maybe she hadn't spent the majority of her life there, but she still felt like the small town was her home.

By the time she returned to her grandmother's house that evening, it was dark out. Marlowe gave her a sleepy squawk of greeting when she walked in the door, and Bunny danced happily around her feet. She bent down to pet the dog before she started barking—her nonna would surely be asleep by now.

"Let's go to the study, Bunny," she whispered to the dog after grabbing a bottle of water from the fridge in the kitchen. "I've still got some work to do."

The dog followed her to her grandfather's study, which was at the end of the front hall. It was a large room with bookshelves on the walls and two big windows, one of which looked out to the forest behind her grandmother's house. There was a wooden perch in front of the other window, where Marlowe sat when Ellie was working in the office during the day; next to the desk was a plush dog bed for Bunny.

The dog went straight to the bed when Ellie opened the door and spun in a tight circle before settling down. Ellie settled herself onto the old leather chair that still smelled faintly of cigars and opened her laptop. She opened the bottle of water and took a sip before rubbing her eyes. It was late, and she was tired. She promised herself she would only work for a few minutes, but if the cheese order wasn't in by early tomorrow morning, the restaurant would miss that week's delivery.

***

She jerked her head up and blinked at the office around her. It took her a second to realize where she was; in her grandfather's study. She must have fallen asleep after emailing the cheese order in. But what had woken her so suddenly? She glanced down and saw that Bunny was on alert as well, her triangular ears pricked and pointed towards the window that looked out into the back yard.

Suddenly she heard a noise that caused goosebumps to rise on her arms. A scream. Bunny let out a sharp bark, and Ellie stood up and rushed over to the window, but with the lights on in the study, all she could see was blackness. She rushed over to the switch by the door, flicked it off, then hurried back to the window. Had the scream been human? It was impossible for her to be sure. She knew that there were probably all sorts of animals in the state park that bordered her grandmother's property… but could any of them make a noise like that?

Ellie pressed her face against the window, peering out. With the lights in the study off, the half-moon's glow shed enough light outside for her to see the outline of the trees on the other side of the yard, but nothing else. The yard was empty.

"It was probably just a fox or something," she said quietly, trying to reassure herself. "Some sort of mating or hunting call."

She was just about to turn away from the window and go to bed when she saw movement along the tree line. She pressed her nose against the cool glass again. *That's no animal*, she thought. *That's a person. And they're coming this way.*

Ellie hurried towards the back door, where the person seemed to be headed. Her heart was pounding, but out of fear for whoever it was, not for herself. Judging by the scream, someone must have gotten hurt. She only hoped that whatever it was, she would be able to help.

She had barely reached the kitchen when something hit the back door, making the wood shake. Ellie was horrified to see bloody hand prints on the glass. She hurried forward and yanked the door open. A woman stumbled inside, a woman that Ellie knew well.

"Shannon?" she gasped, rushing forward to guide her best friend into a chair in the breakfast nook. "What happened? What are you doing out here?"

"I think he's hurt really bad, Ellie," the woman said. She was pale and shaking; her entire front was covered in blood. "You have to come help."

"Who's hurt? Shannon, are you okay? What's going on?"

"A guy I know, Anthony Reeves, he said he wanted to tell me something, a story he found out about. He didn't want anyone to know… we were supposed to meet in secret… Ellie, we have to hurry. He needs help."

"Shannon, I need you to calm down and tell me what's happening," Ellie said. "Should I call an ambulance?"

"No, they won't get here in time. Tony needs help now! The attacker might come back. It could already be too late. Please, Ellie, just help me get him somewhere safe."

As her friend started to cry, Ellie fretted. She didn't know what to do. Waste valuable time calling the police? Go and try to help someone who was gravely injured on her own? And what was this about an attacker?

"How far away is your friend?" she asked at last.

"Just in the woods," Shannon said, getting the words out between sobs. "He's not far…"

"All right," Ellie said with a sigh, throwing her common sense to the wind and deciding to trust that her friend knew best. She was the one that had seen just how badly this Anthony guy was injured, after all. "Lead the way."

CHAPTER THREE

The forest was dark, and even with the flashlight that Ellie had grabbed from a drawer in the kitchen it was difficult to see more than a few yards ahead of them. Nothing outside of the beam of light was visible, and she was beginning to wonder just how her friend knew where they were going when they broke free from the undergrowth and found themselves on a trail.

"He's not too much farther," Shannon whispered. "We were meeting at the crossroads of Eight Mile and Windy Bluffs trails."

This meant nothing to Ellie, who hadn't stepped foot in the state park since moving back. She was already regretting her decision to forgo calling the police—surely she could have spared a couple of minutes to call the emergency line before hurrying out here? To make matters worse, she had been in such a hurry to follow Shannon that she hadn't even thought to bring her cellphone. What if

Anthony, when they found him, was injured badly enough that they weren't able to get him out on their own?

"Just a few more feet," her friend whispered. "There's the marker for the trail."

Suddenly the beam of the flashlight swept over a pair of shoes. Ellie felt a chill as she slowly ran the beam up the pair of legs, revealing a bloodstained torso. She could sense already that something was wrong. No living person could be that still.

At last the beam revealed the pale face of a man with scruffy facial hair and blank, unmoving open eyes. Shannon gave a cry and rushed forward, falling to her knees beside him. Ellie hung back, shaken and feeling sick.

"He's not breathing," Shannon said, her voice high pitched. "Oh my goodness! Ellie, you have to help me. He's not breathing!"

"Shannon…" Ellie said, her voice barely more than a whisper. "Shannon, he's dead."

"He can't be. He was alive when I left him. We just… we just need to give him CPR. Do you know how?"

"He's lost too much blood, that won't help," she told her friend gently. She took a step closer and laid a hand on the other woman's shoulder. "He's gone, Shannon. We have to call the police. Hand me your cellphone, I left mine in the house."

Fumbling, Shannon pulled a phone out of her back pocket and handed it over. She was clutching Anthony's still hand, crying softly. Ellie turned the phone on and punched in the emergency number. The phone tried to send the call through, then flashed a *no service* notification across the screen.

"Crud," Ellie muttered. "Shannon, we have to go back to the house. There's no cell service out here."

"I'm not leaving him," her friend said. It came out almost as a shriek. "It's my fault he was here in the first place."

What do I do now? Ellie thought. *I'm not strong enough to drag a hysterical woman back through the woods. We need the police.*

"I'll go back home and call the sheriff's station, okay?" she said at last. "You just… wait here."

She considered leaving Shannon the flashlight, but knew that she would need it if she had any hope of getting back through the woods alone. Instead, she gave the woman back her phone, then set off alone.

The walk back through the forest was even more nerve-wracking than the journey in had been. She jumped at every sound, and nearly screamed when her pants snared on some thorns. She kept wondering what Shannon had meant by 'attacker.' Had some sort of animal killed Anthony? What could even do that to someone… were there bears in Maine?

Something about the way she said it makes me think that she wasn't talking about an animal when she said that she was worried that the attacker would return, she thought. *And if they were attacked by a person... then he could still be around here somewhere.*

She shuddered and quickened her pace. None of this felt real to her yet. Half an hour ago, she had been napping in her grandfather's study. Was she still dreaming? Was all of this—Shannon appearing at her door covered in blood, the dead man, all of it—just some sort of nightmare?

A branch slipped away from her raised arm and sprang back into her face, whipping her painfully across the cheek. She winced. *Definitely not a dream*, she thought. *It can't be too much further now, can it? I should be out of the forest soon.*

Sure enough, within moments she found herself out of the trees and back in her grandmother's yard. The house looked peaceful, completely at odds with the horror she had just experienced in the forest. Feeling relieved, she made her way through the grass and into the kitchen, blinking in the bright artificial light.

Her cellphone was sitting on the counter next to her purse, where she'd left it when she got home. She grabbed it and, ignoring Bunny, who was sniffing her shoes intently, called the emergency number.

Within an hour, the house was a bustle of activity. After calling the police, Ellie had woken her grandmother to give the woman a chance to get dressed before people began showing up. Sheriff Ward and his two deputies showed up only minutes later, along with an ambulance and a team of paramedics. Ellie did her best to describe the exact spot where she had left Shannon and the dead man, and was relieved when she was told that she should stay in the house. There was no way that she wanted to go back out in that forest.

Then came the waiting. Her grandmother made tea, and the paramedics hovered near the ambulance with their walkie-talkies out. After a few minutes, one of them approached the house and told Ellie that a couple of people from the local search and rescue team were on their way.

"What do you mean?" Ellie asked. "Wasn't Sheriff Ward able to find them? The place where I left Shannon is only a few minutes' walk into the forest, right where those two trails meet. I told him."

"He found the spot, ma'am," the paramedic told her. "But there was no one there."

She felt her stomach drop. Had the person that had attacked Shannon and her friend returned to finish the job? Had he killed Shannon too? But how would one person have had the time to move both bodies?

"They'll find them, ma'am," the paramedic told her, reading the concern on her face. "The local search and rescue group has good dogs. They'll find your friend."

Ellie believed him. She just hoped that they found her alive.

She watched from the window as cars began pulling into her yard. Three different vehicles showed up, and two of them were carrying dogs. Ellie saw a German shepherd and some sort of floppy-eared hound dog get unloaded. Then the three people gathered in a small circle for a moment. Eventually they separated, the two dog-and-handler teams heading towards the forest while the third person approached the front stoop.

"My name is Olivia Malone," she said as they shook hands. She was a serious-looking woman, maybe a decade younger than Ellie, with long black hair was pulled back in a ponytail, and a walkie-talkie clipped to her belt. She looked tired. "I'm the local search and rescue coordinator and trainer. We have two of our best teams out there right now. They'll find Shannon."

"Thanks so much for coming out here," Ellie said. "Come in, you can wait inside. Do you know her?"

"Shannon? She's done a few pieces about my team for the paper. We're acquaintances. She seems like a wonderful woman. Very kind and positive-minded."

"She is," Ellie agreed as Olivia came inside. "She's one of the nicest people I know. I feel so terrible about leaving her out there by herself… but she wouldn't come with me. I didn't know what to do."

"Don't blame yourself. I'm sure you did everything you could. Coming back here and calling the police was the right thing to do. At least we're prepared in case someone is hurt. With two dogs, the sheriff, and two deputies out there searching, it shouldn't take long."

It didn't. Within ten minutes, Olivia's walkie-talkie crackled to life.

"...found...oman," a voice said through the static. "Code green."

"Code green? What does that mean?" Ellie asked. She saw the relief on the other woman's face.

"It means she's alive."

CHAPTER FOUR

An Search and Rescue team had found Shannon wandering deeper into the woods, confused and lost. There was still no sign of Anthony's body, and even when Shannon had calmed down enough to tell her story to the sheriff, she couldn't shed any light on that particular mystery.

"I was waiting with him for you to come back," she said with a glance at Ellie. They were gathered in the kitchen while the search for the body continued. "And then I heard something… footsteps… I was terrified that it was the same person that attacked us before. I ran away without even thinking about where I was going. After a little bit, I began trying to make my way back here, but by then my phone had died and I couldn't see anything at all. It was terrible."

"I'm going to need you to come down to the station with me, Shannon," the sheriff said. "I need to take an official statement, and get a swab of the blood that's on your clothes. Are you sure you aren't injured? Do you want to go to the hospital first?"

The woman shook her head. "All of the blood is Anthony's. I have some scratches from running through the woods, but that's it. I'm ready to go now. The sooner I'm at home with James, the better. Has he been called yet?"

"I let him know as soon as we found you," Russell said. "He'll be waiting at the station."

"All right. Let's get going. Thank you so much, Ellie. I'm sorry for the trouble. I wasn't thinking clearly."

"Don't worry about it, Shannon. I'm just glad you're okay."

"Do you think it would be all right if I thanked the lady whose dog found me?" Shannon asked, directing this question towards Olivia. "Seeing them come out of the darkness towards me… I can't even begin to describe the relief that I felt."

"Of course," Olivia said, smiling. "Her name's Beth, and her dog's name is Niko. They should still be outside. Follow me; I'll introduce you."

Ellie watched out the window as the sheriff, her friend, and Olivia left. The three of them paused next to a woman who was standing by her car with the German shepherd. Shannon shook the woman's hand, then crouched down to pet the dog. Even from this distance, Ellie could see the tears on her friend's face. It had been a crazy night for all of them, but it would have been the worst by far for Shannon—she had witnessed her friend's death, after all. There were still so many mysteries. Who had attacked them? What had happened to that Tony's body? Why hadn't the dogs found him?

She's safe, Ellie thought. *That's the most important thing. Everything else can wait until morning.*

The daylight didn't bring any more answers, however. Ellie, who had suffered through a fitful few hours of sleep after the long and intense night, woke with a pounding headache. She had overslept and was greeted by the screeching of an upset macaw, which didn't help matters any. Marlowe never liked changes of the routine that Ellie had set up over the past few weeks, and the bird, of course, had no idea that there had been a murder.

"I think we still have some of those cinnamon oat muffins that Nonna made the other day," Ellie told the parrot with a sigh as she rubbed her temples. "I'll give you part of one if you promise not to yell anymore."

Marlowe, who knew that word 'muffin,' made a quiet and content squawk and perched next to her food bowl to wait. Bunny followed Ellie into the kitchen, her nails pitter-pattering on the hard floor as she danced around, waiting for muffin crumbs to fall as Ellie broke a piece off for the bird. Deciding that the muffin actually looked pretty good, she stuck the rest of it in the microwave for a few seconds, spread a dollop of butter on top, and ate it standing over the sink. It wasn't the most well-rounded breakfast in the world, but it beat having to cook while she was so out of it.

Still groggy, she brought the piece of muffin back to the bird cage, slipped it through the bars, then started back upstairs to get dressed for the day. She was halfway up when the landline began to ring.

She hesitated, tempted to let the call go to voicemail, but concern for her grandmother got the better of her. The elderly woman was already awake and had gone to water therapy, and Ellie didn't want to chance missing a call from her. With a sigh, she hurried back down the stairs and into the kitchen.

"Hello?"

"Ms. Pacelli?" a male voice asked.

"Yes." Realizing that Ms. Pacelli could mean either her or her grandmother, she quickly added, "This is Eleanora."

"This is Sheriff Ward. I hope I'm not calling too early, but I wanted to catch you before you left for the pizzeria. I'd like to ask you some questions about what happened last night. Do you think you could swing by the station on your way in to work?"

"Oh… sure." She glanced at the stove clock. "How long should it take?"

"Not too long. Plan on about half an hour," he told her.

"All right. I should be there at about ten."

"Perfect. Thank you for your cooperation, Ms. Pacelli."

He hung up, and Ellie slowly put the phone back in its cradle. She should have expected something like this; she had been at the scene of the murder, after all. It was natural for the police to want to ask her some questions. The only problem was that the events of the night before seemed all jumbled up to her now. Her memories of it were a mess of flashing lights and dark trees. It seemed more like a nightmare than like something that had really happened to her. Would she be able to get her thoughts in order in time to give the sheriff the answers he wanted?

CHAPTER FIVE

Kittiport's sheriff's department was located right across from the marina. It was a small building, with none of the security that Ellie had grown used to in the big city. She walked in the door and told the woman behind the desk that she was there to see Sheriff Ward. The woman, Carilyn, asked her to take a seat.

While she was waiting, Ellie checked her phone. She had sent Shannon a text message shortly before heading out the door, asking how she was doing. She had yet to receive an answer.

Though she knew that her friend was likely still recovering from the events of the night before, she couldn't help but feel worried. Shannon was always on her phone, and to go this long without a reply from her felt odd. Was it possible that she had been hurt worse than she'd let on the night before? The thought sent a new spike of anxiety through Ellie. Shannon had been absolutely covered in blood when she saw her. The other woman had insisted that it was all her friend's, but what if she had been lying?

Why would she lie about something like that? Ellie thought. *If she was hurt, why wouldn't she tell me?* She sighed. There were still so many questions she had about the previous night. If luck was with her, Sheriff Ward might be able to answer some of them today.

It wasn't long before a door opened and she was summoned back. The sheriff looked tired, and she suspected that he was wearing the same clothes that he had been wearing last night. *Did he get any sleep?* she wondered.

"Ms. Pacelli. Thanks for stopping in. Will you take a seat?"

She settled herself into one of the worn leather armchairs across the desk from the sheriff's seat. The window behind him looked out into the sheriff's department parking lot, and beyond that the brick side of a dry cleaner's building. It was a bleak view, and she didn't blame him for setting up his office so his back would be to it.

"What can I help you with?" she asked, wondering why she felt nervous. It wasn't like she was a suspect here. "Did you find the body?"

"No," he said. "We're still searching. But if there's a body to be found, we'll find it."

If there's a body to be found? Does he think we're lying about Anthony? She frowned, and was about to ask him aloud when her spoke again.

"Right now I just want you to go over the evening again. Don't leave out any detail, no matter how small. What you saw, what you heard... everything. I'll save my questions until the end—I won't interrupt you unless I need you to repeat something or go deeper into detail about something. Can you do that for me?"

She nodded, then fell silent for a moment to gather her thoughts. At last she began with the moment that she woke up in her grandfather's study and heard the scream.

Telling the story took a while, but Russell remained true to his word and did not interrupt her until she reached the part where she and Shannon found Anthony's body. There he held up a hand to pause the story and asked her questions about the scene. Ellie struggled to remember what the dead man had been wearing, or if there had been any footprints around the body. In the end she answered the questions as best she could, but mentally kicked herself for not remembering more. It was mostly a blur to her now.

Once she had finished telling the story up to the point where he arrived, he began asking her more direct questions. These were easier to answer, and she felt herself relax a bit. It seemed like the worst of it was out of the way.

"Were you aware that Shannon was planning on meeting somebody near your home?"

"What? No, of course not. I had no idea," she said.

"Did you know Anthony Reeves personally?"

"No. I have no idea who he is… or was."

"Why did you leave Shannon at the crime scene when you returned home to call the ambulance?"

"I told you. She was hysterical and wouldn't leave him."

"According to your story, she had already mentioned the attacker at that point. Weren't you worried for her safety?"

"Of course I was," Ellie said, stung. Maybe she hadn't made the smartest decisions last night, but at least she had tried. From the moment she had seen Shannon at her doorway, covered in blood, she had gone into panic mode. Did he really expect her to be thinking clearly? "But she wouldn't leave Anthony, and the cellphone didn't have any service out there. All I could think was that I needed to call an ambulance, or the police… or somebody. Anybody."

He nodded and made a note. "Did you see anybody suspicious on your street earlier that day, or see any signs of anyone else while you were in the woods?"

"No. The only other person I saw was Anthony, and he… well, he had already passed away by the time I got there."

"I see." He made another scribble on his notepad, his brow furrowed. Ellie searched her memory for any other tidbits that might be helpful, but she couldn't think of anything. A glance at her phone showed her that she had to be at the pizzeria in ten minutes. She was just about to ask him if she could take off when she heard raised voices in the hall.

She craned her head around to look towards the door to Russell's office just as it banged open. Standing in the hall was James Ward, Russell's brother and Shannon's husband. His face was beet red, and his fists were clenched.

"What's your problem?" he said, his voice loud. "What're you going after my wife for, Russ?"

"James, calm down," Russell said. His tone was mild, but Ellie could see the muscles in his jaw tense. "I'm not going after anyone. I'm just doing my job."

"She *told* me the sorts of questions you were asking her. I may not have a degree in criminal justice like you do, but I'm not an idiot. You're treating her like a suspect. My *wife*, Russ, and *your* sister-in-law."

"I have to look at her just like I would look at anyone else in this situation. She was the last one to see the body. If there's any chance that she moved it—"

"Shannon can barely lift a bag of dog food on her own! How the heck is she supposed to carry a body?" James slammed his fist into the wall, his teeth gritted. "My wife is innocent, Russell. You'd best quit wasting your time with her and start looking for the real culprit before they come back to finish the job. If she gets hurt, it's on you."

With that, he turned and strode out of the room. Ellie was stunned into silence. She gave Sheriff Ward a wide-eyed look. The few times she had met James since moving back, he had seemed nice and soft-spoken. It was amazing to see the change that came out in him when he was trying to protect his wife.

“He’s a good husband,” Russell said at last, his eyes on the hallway where his brother had been just moments ago. “That, however, was a conversation that should have been held in private. I’m sorry you had to see that.” He heaved a sigh, looking more tired than ever. “You’re free to leave, Ms. Pacelli. I’ll give you a call if I have any more questions.”

CHAPTER SIX

Ellie was running a few minutes behind when she pulled into the lot behind the pizzeria. Despite the fact that she was late, she let the car idle in the parking spot for a few moments while she thought about everything she had heard at the sheriff's department. Did Russell really think his sister-in-law had something to do with the murder? It seemed absurd. *Shannon wouldn't hurt a fly,* she thought. That wasn't even hyperbole—Ellie had actually seen her friend open the door to shoo a fly out instead of swatting it.

I do wonder what she was doing, though, meeting that man out in the woods in the middle of the night, she mused as she shut the engine off. It seemed out of character for her friend. Shannon had mentioned something about a story, and Ellie was bursting with curiosity to find out just what could have been important enough to lure the journalist into the state park at night, but she was determined not to press her friend for answers until the other woman was ready.

"Time to focus on work," she said to herself. "I've got pizzas to sell."

Clara and Rose, the two other female employees at the pizzeria, were both working that day.

"So sorry I'm late," Ellie told them, feeling a stab of guilt for keeping the young women waiting so long. Thank goodness it wasn't a weekend when the pizzeria was busier—there would have been no way that Clara and Rose could have handled it themselves then. "I had the craziest night…"

She told her employees her story as they worked alongside each other, chopping ingredients and grating cheese. By the time she was finished talking, Clara was wearing an amazed look on her face and Rose had stopped all preparations.

"Wow, I can't believe all of that really happened. And they still haven't found the body?"

"Not that I'm aware of," Ellie said. "From what Sheriff Ward said, they were out looking all night."

"That's so weird."

Rose added, “And they have no idea who the killer is, either?”

“None at all, as far as I know.” She was *not* going to mention the fact that Sheriff Ward seemed to be considering that Shannon herself could be a suspect.

“Creepy,” the young woman said with a shudder. “It could be anyone at all, couldn’t it? In a town this small, it’s bound to be someone we know.”

They’re right, Ellie thought, watching her employee begin to spin out a lump of dough. *Unless the killing was completely random, and done by some stranger passing through town, then chances are the murderer is someone I’ve at least seen before.*

The day wore on slowly. Ellie couldn’t focus on her work; she kept thinking over last night instead of paying attention to the pizzas. When she accidentally burnt one of the orders, she finally asked Clara to take over in the kitchen and went out front to sit behind the register. It felt good to be out of the swelteringly warm room. The ovens made the kitchen miserable during the summer, even with the fans running, and though it was the tail end of the season, today was an unseasonably warm day. The dining area, by contrast, was pleasantly cool thanks to the air conditioning, and Ellie breathed a sigh of relief as she tilted her face up towards the vent. She would switch with Clara again in a bit, but she was going to enjoy this while she could.

She straightened up when the bell above the pizzeria's door jingled. The woman walking into the restaurant was none other than Shannon. Ellie blinked in surprise, then offered her friend a wide smile.

"I wasn't expecting to see you for a while," she said, waving her friend over. A family was sitting at one of the booths in the far corner, but if they spoke quietly, Ellie doubted that they would be overheard.

"Technically I'm supposed to be at home today, recuperating, but James was driving me crazy," Shannon sighed, leaning on the counter. Her left arm was held up in a sling.

"I thought you weren't seriously hurt, Shannon," Ellie said, her brows drawing together in concern for her friend. "If whoever attacked your friend got you, too, then you should listen to your doctor and stay home. I wouldn't have let you go out in the woods again if I had known."

"Oh, this?" The woman lifted her arm with a wince. "It's a sprain, that's all. From when I was trying to find my way out of the woods."

Ellie bit her lip. Her friend wasn't meeting her eyes, but she didn't see why she would lie about something like this. *She must be in pain*, she thought. *People act differently when they're hurting.*

"I'm sorry. I hope it heals quickly," she said at last. "I never should have left you alone out there."

"It's not your fault—I told you to, remember? Anyway, let's talk about something else. I've been talking about last night all day, first to James, then to the sheriff. Russell kept trying to get me to remember more and more. I finally had to tell him that no matter how many times he asks me, I'm not going to suddenly remember that the guy who attacked us had a mole under his left eyebrow. It was dark, and he was wearing a hood. That's all I know."

"He's just trying to be thorough," Ellie said. "He made me repeat stuff a bunch of times when he questioned me, too. He's very detail-oriented; he must be good at his job."

Her friend opened her mouth to reply, but was interrupted when Clara stepped through the door to the kitchen.

"Oh—sorry, Ms. Pacelli. I didn't mean to interrupt, but Clayton is here and he needs you to sign for the delivery. He's got to make a fish delivery soon, and can't wait much longer."

"Clayton… can you remind me what he does again, Clara? Is he the guy that delivers the boxes?"

"Cheese," Clara said. "Lisa does the boxes. She comes all the way from Portland, remember?"

"I'm getting there," Ellie said with a chuckle. "Clayton delivers cheese, Lisa does boxes. I'll have it down eventually. Go ahead and send him through."

Clara disappeared back into the kitchen, and her spot was taken a moment later by a young man with messy blond hair and a crooked smile.

"My uncle added a free sample of his new bacon-flavored cheddar," he told Ellie as he handed her his clipboard to sign. "It's half-off all this month if you want to order more."

"Thanks, Clayton," she said, scribbling her signature on the line he indicated. "I'll try some later today. It sounds pretty good, but I'm not sure how well it would go on a pizza."

"Probably pretty well," he said with a grin as he took the clipboard back from her. "Who doesn't like bacon? Anyway, thanks for signing and I'm sorry for the interruption. I've gotta run. We lost one of our employees recently, and everyone's working double."

She told him goodbye and wished him luck. Once he went back into the kitchen, she turned back to Shannon. She was surprised to see her friend's brows drawn together in a frown. Ellie looked around behind herself to make sure that Clayton had gone, then asked, "What is it?"

"I just feel like I know that guy from somewhere," her friend said. "Is he a local?"

"I think he lives in the next town over. At least, that's where his uncle's business is," Ellie said.

"I must be going crazy," Shannon said with a laugh. She shook her head. "Anyway, before I forget… I wanted to invite you to dinner at my house this weekend. James is having a few of his friends over to watch a game, and I could use some female company. Aaand… two of them are single."

Ellie chuckled. "Well, I'm not really looking to date right now—it hasn't exactly gone very well for me in the past. But I'd be happy to come over and spend some girl time together. Should I bring anything for the meal?"

"James is cooking, and I'm not sure what exactly he has planned, but chips and dip are always popular with that crew. Don't worry about it if you don't have time, though."

"I'll see if my grandmother has any good dip recipes for game day," Ellie told her friend. "Thanks for the invite. I'm looking forward to it."

CHAPTER SEVEN

"It's such a beautiful day, isn't it, dear?" Ann Pacelli asked, fluffing her curls with one hand as she gazed out across the bay. "I only wish I didn't get so dreadfully sick on boats. It's a pity to keep the *Eleanora* docked on a day like this."

"Have you tried any medicine for seasickness?" Ellie asked her grandmother. "I'm sure there's something that would work for you."

"Oh, I've tried everything." The elderly woman sighed. "The sea just isn't for me. I do love walking out here, though. Thanks for joining me, Ellie."

"Of course. It's a great morning for a walk, and it's nice to be able to see more of the town. I spend most of my time cooped up at the pizzeria or at home. I'm sure Bunny appreciates getting out, too."

The little dog was prancing a few steps ahead of them, her thin leather leash looped loosely around her owner's wrist. The papillon couldn't have been happier—it was a busy morning at the marina, and there was no shortage of fascinating smells to investigate.

"I never liked little dogs much," her grandmother mused as she watched the little black-and-white dog poke her nose at an inquisitive seagull. "But Bunny has me wrapped around her paw."

Ellie smiled. "She knows how to get what she wants, that's for sure. How could anyone say no to that little face?"

The paused by the *Eleanora* for a few minutes, admiring the boat's flawless white paint and reminiscing about Ellie's grandfather. Arthur Pacelli had been a man of hobbies: boating, fishing, cooking pizza, and building wooden models had been some of his favorite pastimes. The pizzeria had started out as a retirement hobby, but it had taken on a life of its own and within a year of its opening, it had become a full-time job for him.

It must have been hard for him to step back from managing the pizzeria after all those years, Ellie thought as she gazed at the boat that had been named after her. For seventeen years her grandfather had tended to his restaurant day in and day out. He had only begun taking more time away from it two years before his death. *I really wish I had come back here to visit before he died.* She would always regret that, but took some solace in the knowledge that she was doing just what he would have wanted her to do—managing the pizzeria and taking care of her grandmother.

Bunny tugged on the leash, distracting her from her thoughts. Ellie looked down, and saw that the dog was focused intently on a young seagull that was perched on the edge of the *Eleanora.* The brown and white speckled bird either didn't fear dogs or knew that the papillon was restricted by her leash, because it sat still and unruffled on the boat's bow even as the dog began to yip.

"Bunny, come on… stop that," Ellie said. "It's just a bird."

The dog ignored her and jumped forward again, only to be stopped at the edge of the dock by the leash. Ellie was just about to reach down and scoop her up when Bunny twisted around and with a shake of her head, backed out of her collar. In a blink, the dog had leapt off the dock towards the boat. The distance was too far for her little legs, and she landed with a splash in the water. The bird took off, startled by the sound, and Ellie fell to her knees, looking into the water with terror.

"Bunny?" she called out. Her grandmother peered over the edge next to her.

"There she is!" she said a moment later when the little dog surfaced. Ellie reached for her, but the dock was too high above the water. The papillon swam towards the boat, even farther out of her grasp, and began pawing at the side in a desperate attempt to get up and out of the water.

"Oh my goodness," Ellie said, looking around frantically for something she could use to get the dog back onto the dock. Almost everyone who docked their boat at the marina was a fisher—weren't there any nets? "Bunny, just keep swimming. I'll get you out, I promise."

She was about to step over to the boat, thinking that she might be able to reach her dog better there, when a strong hand gripped her shoulder.

"Let me."

Ellie turned to see none other than Russell Ward standing behind her. He was wearing a fishing vest and had a pole on the dock behind him. She had forgotten that his boat was docked near the *Eleanora*.

He must have decided to get some morning fishing in before heading to work.

She stepped back and watched as he lowered himself into the water, keeping one hand firmly gripping the wooden supports of the dock, and extending the other towards the dog.

"Come here," he said. "Come here, pup."

"Her name's Bunny," Ellie said, watching breathlessly as a wave washed over the dog's head.

"Here, Bunny."

The bedraggled papillon turned away from the boat and began paddling toward the sheriff. She struggled through the water until Russell was finally able to grab her. He pulled her over and handed her up to Ellie before climbing back onto the dock himself.

"Thank you so much," she told him, hugging the cold and dripping-wet dog to her chest. "She slipped out of her collar, and she's never been swimming before. I was so worried."

"Glad to help," Russell said. "Is she okay?"

"I think so. Just surprised and cold. I'm sorry you got all wet, too."

His jeans were sopping, and Ellie knew from experience that even after they dried they'd be encrusted in salt.

"Don't worry about it. I keep extra clothes on the boat." He looked down at the puddle he was standing in and chuckled. "It's not the first time I've had to jump in and save someone's dog, and it was a lot easier hauling a Chihuahua out of the marina than it is hauling a lab out of the ocean."

"Papillon," she corrected automatically. "But thanks again."

"Well, you two have a nice day, Ms. Pacelli… Ann." He shook Ellie's grandmother's hand, and just nodded to Ellie since her arms were full of Bunny. "I'll be seeing you around. You're coming to dinner Saturday night, aren't you?"

She nodded, surprised. She hadn't been expecting him to be there, but it made sense. He was James's brother, after all.

"Do you watch sports?"

"No, not really," she told him. "I just thought it would be nice to go, since Shannon invited me."

"I'm sure she'll be glad to have another woman around to talk to. I'll see you Saturday, Ms. Pacelli. Now go get that poor dog warmed up." He nodded to her again, bent to pick up his fishing pole, and left.

"Well wasn't that just something?" her grandmother asked as they walked back up the dock together. "It was quite the rescue, wasn't it?"

"It was very nice of him," Ellie agreed. "I feel so bad. I just froze. Poor Bunny." She cuddled the dog, who was shivering in her arms.

"She'll be fine once she gets dried off and warmed up. We'll go right home, and I'll make her some warm chicken broth while you towel her off."

"Thanks, Nonna." Ellie smiled over at her grandmother, glad that they were getting a chance to develop a real relationship after so many years of no communication but Christmas and birthday cards.

"Watch out!"

Both women jumped back at the shout. Just feet in front of them, a flood of silvery fish washed over the dock.

"Crap," the man said, jumping from his boat to the solid wood. "Devon, you did it again! Get out here and clean up this mess, and learn how to tie a good knot already."

He cleared his throat and turned to face them. Ellie realized what an odd trio they must look like, with a sopping wet dog carried in her arms.

"Sorry about that," he grunted. "I can't find a good crew worth anything these days. Hold on, I'll help you through."

He kicked fish aside until he had formed a sort of path through the mess, then stood aside and gestured for them to walk through. A teenager had appeared, and was trying to scoop the fish back into the net that they had fallen out of. Careful to avoid the slimy carcasses, Ellie and Ann walked by with wrinkled noses, the older woman gripping her granddaughter's arm for support. As they passed by the boat, Ellie saw the words *Green Mermaid* on the side.

"Thanks," she said to the man when they were through. He looked slightly familiar, but she couldn't figure out why. "Sorry about your fish."

"Eh, it'll be fine. We lost a few, but the rest can still go to market… if Devon hurries up and gets them in the cart." He said the last part more loudly, looking back over his shoulder at his young assistant before turning back to Ellie and her grandmother. "You two ladies have a nice day, now."

I'm beginning to think the marina's a dangerous place to be, Ellie thought as she, her grandmother, and the wet dog continued their perilous walk back to the car. *That was two close calls within minutes of each other. Thank goodness we're all okay.*

CHAPTER EIGHT

Ellie loved Saturday mornings. During the week, her commitment was to the pizzeria. She scheduled herself to work every day, Monday through Friday, and most of the time was there from before the restaurant opened until after it closed. As the boss, she had the freedom to pick and choose her hours, but she rarely took advantage of it. What else would she do, if she wasn't at work? Besides, she enjoyed being a part of the pulse of the restaurant and having a hand in the day to day business of it.

Still, she loved weekends. Saturday mornings came with a feeling of freedom—she had a whole two days to do whatever she wanted. She might stop by the pizzeria, and usually did, but she didn't *have* to.

That feeling of freedom usually faded as the day wore on and she turned her attention to the long list of chores waiting for her attention. Grocery shopping, cleaning the bathroom, mopping the floor under Marlowe's cage—the bird loved throwing her food between the bars when she got bored—the little jobs were endless. She usually spent all day Saturday putting off the worst of the chores, then spent Sunday doing her best to catch up on the list before the work week started again. It was a cycle that she couldn't seem to break free of, no matter how hard she tried.

This Saturday was different. She woke up in a good mood, and that mood stayed with her as she worked her way down the list. Scrubbing the bars of Marlowe's cage? No problem. The macaw hung out on the banister, watching her closely while she cleaned. Laundry? No complaints from her. She needed something clean to wear to dinner that night, anyway. Grocery shopping? Well, she needed to buy the ingredients for the dip, after all.

She was still in a good mood when she got back from the store and started a pot of water boiling on the stove for chicken breasts. Humming to herself, she began to dice onions on the cutting board while she waited for the water to heat up.

"You sound happy," her grandmother said as she walked into the room and set her purse down on the table. "What are you cooking? Is that for lunch, because I'm starved."

"This is the dip for tonight," Ellie told her. "I'll make extra for you, though. How was your hair appointment?"

"Good, as always. I've got my curls for another week. You know, I bet Darshan could do something with *your* hair if you wanted."

"I don't think I'm a curly-haired sort of woman," Ellie said with a chuckle. "I'll make do with my straight hair. It certainly doesn't require much maintenance."

"Well, whatever you think is best, dear. Just let me know if you want to set up an appointment. She doesn't *just* do curls, you know. You could just go in for a trim and some layering."

"I'll think about it, Nonna. Right now I want to focus on cooking. I don't want to mess this up."

"You spend all day cooking, don't you? You should be a pro by now."

Ellie laughed as she put the chicken breasts into the pot of boiling water. "Making dip is a bit different from making pizzas. And I'm nowhere near being an expert at that. Papa had years of experience. I've got less than two months."

"Well, I think you do a marvelous job, dear." Her grandma gave her a whiskery kiss on the cheek, then opened the fridge to grab an iced tea. "I'll let you work in peace. In an hour or so I'll come out and make sandwiches for us—and get a taste of some of that dip you're making."

By the time evening rolled around, Ellie was beginning to get a flutter of anxiety in her stomach whenever she looked at the clock. The dip was finished and in the fridge; it would be easy enough to heat it up on the stove at Shannon's house. The bags of chips were sitting on the counter, ready to go. She was wearing her favorite pair of jeans and a black blouse, both of which smelled fresh and flowery from the laundry detergent. All she had to do when it was time to leave would be to slip on her shoes and put everything in the car. So why did she keep pacing from room to room and double-checking her makeup in the mirror?

Is this because Shannon told me two of the men that will be there are single? she wondered. *I don't even want to date right now, so why on earth am I checking my lipstick for the third time in a row?*

"You look fine, my dear," her grandmother said from the hallway as she walked back towards the kitchen to begin putting the food in the car. "Sheriff Ward won't be able to take his eyes off of you."

"What?" Ellie squeaked, stopping in her tracks. "What are you talking about?"

"Well you're going to dinner with him, aren't you?" the old woman asked.

"No, no, I'm just going to hang out with Shannon while her husband and some of his friends watch a game on TV," she told her grandmother.

"Okay, if you say so," Ann said with a mischievous grin. "Though I can't remember the last time I kept checking my makeup every ten minutes before spending time with my girlfriends."

"I just want to make a good impression," Ellie said. "I'll be meeting some of James's friends, and if they're friends with Jeffrey too, then they probably already have a poor idea of me."

Jeffrey Dunham was the owner of Cheesaroni Calzones, Papa Pacelli's main competitor. He had taken an instant dislike to Ellie, and the feeling was mutual. She felt a stab of panic as she realized that he might be there. She most definitely did *not* want to spend the night trying to ignore barbed comments from him.

"Oh, they'll all love you, dear. That man's just jealous that you did such a good job with your grandfather's restaurant. Don't give him a second thought."

Ellie smiled, thankful for the kind words, and gave her grandmother a hug goodbye. With her purse over her shoulder and her arms full of food, she walked towards the front door, saying goodbye to Marlowe as she passed her cage and gently nudging Bunny back inside when she tried to slip out behind her. The little dog had made a full recovery from her spill in the harbor a few days ago, and seemed eager to go on her next adventure.

"I'll see all of you later," she said as she shut the door behind her. "Don't wait up for me, Nonna. And can you lock the door after I'm gone? My hands are too full."

Shannon greeted her at the door, looking happier than she had since the night of the murder. She helped Ellie carry the chips and dip inside, then handed her a glass of wine.

"Dinner is still on the grill, but we should be ready to eat soon," she said. "The guys are all outside. Do you want to join them?"

"Might as well," Ellie said, taking a sip from the wine glass. "We should at least get the introductions out of the way."

She followed her friend outside and waited while the other woman introduced her to the three men that she didn't know. Harris was about her age and balding; he was quick to smile, and was happily married. His wife, Ellie gathered, usually watched the game with them, but was out of town at the moment. Carter and Isaac were the two single men that Shannon had told her about earlier in the week. As she greeted them, Ellie wondered whether Shannon had set this whole thing up on purpose to try to find her a date. Her friend was well meaning, but a bit too nosy for her own good. *No wonder she ended up being a journalist,* she thought. *It's the perfect job for her.*

"And of course you know James and Russell," Shannon finished.

"Hey Ellie, glad you could make it," James said. He was standing at an expensive-looking grill which was loaded with hamburgers, bratwurst, and chicken breasts.

"Thanks for inviting me," Ellie said. "The barbecue smells great."

"And it'll taste even better," he said. "I don't want to sound full of myself, but the Ward family secret sauce is to die for."

"And very secret," Shannon added with a laugh. "He won't even tell me how he makes it."

"I told you I'd give you the recipe if you learned how to grill without burning everything," he said, giving her a fond grin. "It's a sauce that's supposed to go on meat—not charcoal."

Ellie took another sip of her wine as everyone laughed and felt herself relax. No Jeffrey, and everyone seemed nice. This was turning out to be a great night.

CHAPTER NINE

Dinner was a casual affair. James brought in all of the grilled meat from outside and put it on big platters while Shannon got the potato salad, watermelon, and condiments out of the fridge and Ellie began heating the dip up on the stove. The gooey, cheesy concoction smelled delicious, and she couldn't wait for people to try it. She had used some of the bacon-flavored cheddar from the cheese shipment, along with cream cheese, shredded chicken, a dab of hot sauce, and green onions. She had tried some earlier, and it had been scrumptious.

Once all of the food was ready, people grabbed plates and served themselves, all sitting around the big table. Ellie ended up between Russell and Shannon, and was interested to see a new side to the usually serious sheriff as he laughed with his brother.

"Great dip, Ellie," he said partway through the meal, turning to her. "How's that little dog of yours doing?"

"She's great," she told him. "Thank you again. I don't know what would have happened if you hadn't come along."

"I'm sure you would have figured something out," he said. "Glad to hear she's doing well, though."

Ellie was itching to ask him about the case. Had they found the body yet? Did they have any idea who the killer was? It had happened practically in her backyard, after all. She knew that it wasn't exactly a polite conversation to have at the dinner table, however, and forced herself to wait. She would try asking Shannon about it after dinner instead.

Once the meal was finished, the guys helped clear the table before heading into the living room to watch the game. Ellie followed Shannon into the kitchen, where she was getting started on the dishes.

"Need help?" she asked.

"Nah, I'm just soaking them. James will help me wash everything in the morning. He always says he feels bad if I do them on my own, since they're his friends."

“He seems like a great guy,” Ellie said, a touch wistfully. “You’re lucky.”

“He really is.” She looked up, a smile on her face. “I love him just as much now as I did on the day we got married. Maybe even more, after all we’ve been through together. I really hope you can find someone like that one day, Ellie. Not all guys are jerks.”

Ellie knew that her friend was referencing Kenneth Aubrey, her fiancé. She had found out that he was having an affair a few months ago, and had called off their engagement. He had been her boss as well as the man that she was going to marry, and had taken full advantage of his position by firing her the day after she gave him back his ring. It had been the worst, most humiliating week of Ellie’s life, and she still winced whenever she thought back on it.

“What do you think about Carter and Isaac?” her friend asked after a moment.

“Well, they both seem nice. I haven’t really gotten much of a chance to talk to either of them.” She hesitated. “Shannon… I’ve been wondering some things about, you know, that night.”

Her friend paused for a moment, then continued scraping the dishes into the garbage can. "Go ahead. But I haven't remembered anything new."

"It's nothing like that. I guess the main thing I've been wondering is who exactly was Anthony? Why were you meeting him there, in the woods behind my house? I know you said it was for a story, but what *sort* of story?"

Shannon sighed. "All of this started before you even moved here. A couple of months back, some people got pretty sick from eating bad fish served at a few restaurants around town. One older man actually died from it. There was a big outcry, and all of the restaurants were inspected. Some of us at the *Kittiport Times* have been investigating up the supply chain, trying to figure out what happened and call the people out. No one really made much progress, and I had pretty much given up on finding anything out until Anthony Reeves stepped forward. We were friends back in school—I don't know if you remember him, he was in the band and played the drums—anyway, he told me he knew what happened. I guess he knows the person responsible for it personally, and had a falling out with them or something. He was just about to tell me who it was when we got attacked." She grimaced. "I feel horrible saying it, but I can't stop thinking about how I'll probably never know what happened now that he's dead. I think I'll give things some time to settle down, then start digging around in his employment history. Maybe someone he worked for was involved."

"Wow," Ellie said. "Someone died from bad fish? That's a pretty big deal. I mean, it could wreck someone's business if it got out that they were responsible. Do you think that whoever he was about to betray is the one that killed him?"

"I'm sure of it," Shannon said. "What other motive could there be?"

"Does the sheriff know about all of this?" she asked, glancing towards the living room.

"Yeah. I told him about it as soon as I calmed down enough to gather my thoughts." The other woman sighed. "I know it sounds stupid, but I keep going through my notes to see if there's any clue about who was behind the fish incident. I feel like if I can solve that, then I can solve the murder and Anthony's family will finally get some peace."

"Was he married?" Ellie asked.

Shannon nodded. "He had a wife and two kids. Young girls, if I remember right."

"Wow," Ellie said, feeling sick. "I can't imagine what this is like for them."

"Me either," her friend said, looking sad. "Anthony was a good guy. The world is worse off without him."

Ellie and Shannon went outside after that, drinking wine and talking about happier things. *It's nice to have someone to reminisce with*, she thought as she gazed up at the stars with her friend. Back in Chicago, she had never really found the time to do this—to just kick back and relax. She wanted to make a habit of it now that she had the time.

The two women were interrupted in their conversation when the back door slid open and Russell stepped out onto the porch. He was holding his cellphone at his side, and looked grim.

"There you are," he said to them. "I've been looking for you. I've got news."

"What is it?" Shannon asked, setting her glass of wine down and turning in her seat. Ellie followed suit, feeling an anxious flutter in her stomach. Whatever it was, it couldn't be good.

"The body's been found," he said. "In the river, by a high schooler walking her dog."

She winced. *That poor girl's going to have nightmares for a long time*, she thought.

"Oh my goodness," her friend said, clapping a hand over her mouth. "How did the body get to the river?"

"The killer probably came back and moved it in an effort to cover his or her tracks," the sheriff said. He shoved the cellphone back into his pocket. "I've got to head to the station. If either of you remember anything more, please give me a call. The killer would have had to move the body between when Shannon got lost in the woods and when we got there. That's only about a fifteen-minute span, and there can't have been many people nearby at the time. Someone has to have seen the killer. We just have to find out who and get them to come in and report it."

He went back inside, leaving Ellie and Shannon alone on the porch. The two women exchanged a glance. Their mellow good mood was wrecked.

"I should get going, too," Ellie said after a moment. "It's late, and I'm getting tired. I had a nice time, though."

"Me too," Shannon sighed. "I know it's good that they found the body, but I kind of wish it could have waited until morning. Now I'm going to be thinking about it all night."

"Me too. I hope the killer gets caught soon. It's weird to think all of this happened right behind my grandmother's house." She stood up and stretched, then looked down at her friend. Something that she sheriff had said struck her. The killer would have had only a short span of time to move the body—just minutes, really. What were the chances that he had come back at just the right time to avoid running into Shannon? Was it possible that her friend knew more than she was saying?

CHAPTER TEN

After a restless Sunday at home waiting for more news about the murder, Ellie decided to head into the pizzeria early on Monday. Work, she decided, was the best way to take her mind off of things. Besides, she wanted to experiment with some new toppings before her employees got there for the day. The bacon-flavored cheese had tasted wonderful in the dip; she wondered how it would work on pizza.

She fired up the ovens when she got to the pizzeria and started work immediately. She began by getting a ball of thick-crust dough out of the fridge and kneading and spinning it out like Xavier had shown her all those weeks ago when she first moved back. After putting it in the oven to pre-bake she began preparing the toppings: bacon bits, mushroom, and green peppers. For the cheese she decided to go mostly with the normal mozzarella, with a little of the shredded smoky bacon cheddar cheese. By the time she got everything ready, the crust had baked long enough to be ready for the sauce and toppings.

She dolloped the sauce on first, smoothing it out with the back of a spoon, then added a generous amount of shredded cheese. Next she tossed the toppings on, doing her best to spread them evenly over the cheese. She finished by taking a handful of the shredded bacon cheddar and sprinkling it on the crust, hoping that it would bake in and give the pizza crust a nice, smoky flavor.

"If you taste as good as you look, I'll add you to the menu," she said. Then she realized she was talking to a pizza, and pressed her lips together. *Talking to pets is one thing,* she thought as she put the pizza in the oven, amused at herself. *Talking to your food is a whole different ballgame.*

She made a few more pizzas for the early lunch crowd. Then, while the pizzas cooked, she puttered around the restaurant, dusting the corners and performing the small chores that needed to be done every day before opening. She finished just as the pizza was ready to come out of the oven and smiled, proud of herself. She was getting so much better at all of this.

This pizza looked and smelled good, which was promising. The cheese on the edges of the crust was a nice golden brown, and she felt her stomach growl at the sight of it. She had skipped lunch purposefully for this—hopefully it was worth the wait. If the flavors ended up going together well, she would add a larger amount of the bacon cheddar cheese to their next order, and Clayton and his uncle would be happy.

"Time to slice you," she said, before realizing that she was talking to food once again. *I've really got to stop that,* she thought as she grabbed the pizza cutter. *It's a bit creepy, really. I clearly need to get out more.*

At long last she sat down at the employees' table in the back of the kitchen with a slice of the ooey, gooey cheese-smothered pizza. She blew cautiously on it before taking a bite, having burnt her tongue on hot pizza one too many times to be reckless when it came to eating a slice right out of the oven.

Once she deemed it was cool enough to bite safely, she tasted it. As she chewed, she smiled. It was tasty. More than tasty, really. It was delicious. The only problem with it was that it was slightly too salty, but in retrospect, that was to be expected of a pizza with bacon as a topping and bacon-flavored cheese. She would have to change that next time, but with a few tweaks she was certain that she could put this pizza on the menu after their next cheese order.

“Good job, Clayton,” she said softly, just as the employee door opened and Jacob came in.

“Hey, Ms. Pacelli,” he said. “Am I late? It smells amazing in here.”

“No, you’re not late. I’m early. I wanted to try out something new. Here, grab a slice if you want and tell me what you think.”

Jacob and Rose, who tried a slice of the pizza when she arrived a few minutes later, were fans of it. Ellie grinned when Rose told her that it would be even better with thin crust. Ellie was glad. Both employees had been here longer than she had, and despite their young age, she valued their opinions. They knew the customers better than she did, so she was prepared to take them at their word when they said the pizza would be a hit. But she’d stick with the thick crust for a while.

Ellie volunteered to stay in the kitchen for the first part of the day, letting Rose take what was generally regarded as the best job—watching the register—while Jacob handled deliveries. It was an unusually busy day for a Monday, and Ellie was on a roll. She had finally gotten to the point where she knew how to make most of the pizzas without checking the recipe binder, which she was quite proud of.

Despite the fact that she enjoyed cooking, the heat from the ovens was decidedly unpleasant. She understood why her employees complained about it so much, and why working the register was so popular, so she was surprised when Rose came into the kitchen an hour before they were due to switch spots.

"There's a lady out front that wants to see you, Ms. Pacelli. I think she's a reporter or something," the young woman said, flicking her long hair back over her shoulder and eyeing the hairnets hanging on the wall with resignation. "She's got a notebook and stuff, so it'll probably take a while. I'll start working back here, I guess."

"Thanks, Rose," Ellie said, removing her own hairnet and heading over to the sink to wash her hands. "You can have an extra hour up front later this evening if you want."

After she cleaned herself up a bit, she pushed through the swinging kitchen door to the dining area. She was expecting to see Shannon, so she was completely shocked to see another woman, especially one that she didn't recognize.

"Hi, I'm Chloe McCullough, reporter for the *Kittiport Times*," she said, extending her hand. "You must be Ellie Pacelli?"

"I really prefer Eleanora, though most people call me Ellie," Ellie said, shaking the other woman's hand. "How can I help you?"

"I'm investigating the murder of Anthony Reeves and trying to figure out how it ties in with an incident involving bad fish from a few months ago," the reporter said. "Shannon is a colleague of mine, and I know you two are close. I was wondering if you might have some insight into what happened?"

"I… I don't, sorry. I don't know anything more than anyone else," Ellie said. She bit her lip, knowing that she wasn't telling the full truth. She had spoken to Shannon privately a few times, of course, and there was also the news about the body being found… but surely if the sheriff wanted that to be public knowledge, he would have put it in the paper.

"Well," the reported said, sounding disappointed. "I'm sorry to hear that. The people of Kittiport deserve to read the truth, Ms. Pacelli. But the truth seems elusive in this case."

She has a point, Ellie thought as she watched Chloe leave. *No one seems to know what happened, or why. Did I do the right thing by turning her away? Or would talking to her have helped shed light on some answers at last?*

CHAPTER ELEVEN

Ellie was about to go back into the kitchen to give Rose her last hour up front at the register when the bell above the door jingled and someone she recognized came in. It took her a moment to realize why the man was so familiar.

"You," she said before she could help herself when she realized who it was. "You're the guy who spilled fish on my grandmother and me at the marina the other day."

"Technically, that was my assistant," the man said with a sheepish grin. "But still, I suppose I owe you an introduction. Shawn Franks, at your service."

"Eleanora Pacelli," Ellie said. "It's nice to officially meet you."

"Same," he said. "So, do you own this joint?"

"My grandfather did, and I suppose now my grandmother does," she told him. "I just run it. Anyway… what can I get you? We've got a lunch combo going on until two. Two slices and a drink from the fridge for six dollars."

"Yeah, I'll take that if you've got Hawaiian," he said.

"Sure do. It'll be just a minute."

She rang him up and ducked into the kitchen to tell Rose his order. While she was back there she heard the bell above the door jingle again, marking yet another customer. *We're really busy today*, she thought, smiling to herself. She returned to the register to find Clara standing in line behind Shawn with Clayton, the delivery guy, at her side.

"I'm surprised to see you here on your day off," she told her employee. "Nice to see you again, by the way, Clayton."

"This *is* the best pizza place in town," Clara pointed out. "Do you expect us to eat at Cheesaroni Calzones?"

"You've got a point," Ellie said with a smile.

"How'd you like that bacon cheddar cheese, Ms. P?" Clayton asked.

"It was great, actually," she told him. "I used it in some buffalo dip, and I tried it out on a pizza this morning. I'll be adding it to our next order."

"Awesome," he said with a grin.

The kitchen door opened and Rose handed a small box over to Ellie. "Two slices of Hawaiian," she said.

"Here you go, Mr. Franks," Ellie said, handing the box off to the fisherman. "Go ahead and grab your drink out of the fridge. Have a nice lunch."

Rose waited until the customer had left, then turned to Clara with her eyebrows raised. "What're you doing here?"

"Why does everyone keep asking that?" the bushy-haired young woman asked, exasperated. "I'm not allowed to visit when I'm not scheduled for a shift? I happen to be a paying customer at the moment. I ordered a barbecue chicken pizza about half an hour ago."

"That was you? I thought the last name was familiar. It's ready—it's in the warming rack. Hold on, I'll go get it."

The blonde woman vanished back into the kitchen, still shaking her head as if unable to believe the fact that someone would actually choose to come into work on a day that they didn't have to. Ellie chuckled. She and her three employees had gotten off to a bumpy start, but now that she had gotten a chance to know them, she found that she honestly liked each of them.

"Do you have a bathroom?" Clayton asked her suddenly.

"Oh, yeah. It's that door next to the drinks fridge. We just haven't gotten the new sign for it yet," she told him.

"Thanks."

He had just shut the door when Rose returned, carrying the pizza. She glanced around the dining area and, seeing that Clayton wasn't in the room, leaned across the counter conspiratorially.

"Are you two… dating?" the young woman asked her friend in a low voice. Ellie couldn't help but listen in, and had to admit that she was curious about the answer herself.

"Sort of," Clara said back, keeping her own voice low. "He just asked me out last night. We're hanging out today, and we're having dinner at the White Pine Kitchen on Thursday at eight."

"Nice," Rose said, drawing out the word and giving a low whistle. "He's cute. Who does he work for again? Is it his uncle or his brother?"

"His uncle," Clara said. "He owns East Coast Delivery and Cold Storage. It's a mouthful, but I guess they've got branches all over Maine. It seems like a pretty successful business. Clayton makes good money, and all he has to do is drive that truck around and deliver stuff."

"That sounds pretty easy. Maybe I should think about switching jobs." Rose seemed to suddenly realize that her boss was standing just feet away, and quickly backpedaled. "Just kidding, Ms. Pacelli. I mean, I love working here."

Ellie gave the girl a mock frown, then grinned. "I know you do, Rose, don't worry," she said, struggling not to laugh. To Clara, she added, "Good luck on your date. I hope everything goes well for the two of you. He seems like a nice guy."

"Thanks, Ms. Pacelli," Clara said, blushing.

The bathroom door opened and Clayton rejoined them, casting a suspicious look over the two young women when they both burst into fits of laughter.

"What did I miss?" he asked.

"Nothing," Clara said, grinning. "Come on, let's get going. I'm starved."

Rose shook her head as the young couple walked out the door together. "Can you believe that?" she asked. "I'm a little bit jealous. Clayton is cute."

"I think he and Clara go very well together," Ellie said. "Don't worry, you'll find someone, too."

"You think?" the young woman chewed on her lip, still gazing at the door. "I dunno. All of the guys I've dated lately have been jerks."

"It just takes time to find the right person," she told her employee. "But I think there's someone out there for everyone."

"You really believe that?"

Ellie thought for a moment. "Yeah, I suppose I do," she said at last. "But in the meantime, we've got work to do. I'll head back into the kitchen for another hour like I promised, but I want you to sweep the floors and wash the windows while you're out front."

"Maybe I should become a delivery driver," Rose grumbled as she headed towards the supply closet. "You don't have to sweep trucks."

CHAPTER TWELVE

Ellie woke to laughter early the next morning. Utterly confused, she sat up in bed and blinked. Bunny was still curled up on the pillow next to her, soundly asleep; although how she could be sleeping through that racket was anyone's guess. The sounds of hysterical laughter increased to a pitch that she realized could only be produced by one member of the household: Marlowe.

"What is going on with that bird?" she muttered. At Ellie's words, the dog next to her perked up, and began wagging her tail. She sighed. She knew that even if Marlowe fell quiet, there would be no getting back to sleep now that Bunny was awake, too. It looked like it was just going to have to be an early morning for her.

She got out of bed, put on her robe and slippers, and opened the bedroom door. The papillon darted down the stars ahead of her. Ellie followed more slowly, still feeling groggy with sleep. As she descended the stairway and came into view of the birdcage, the red macaw fell silent.

“What was so funny?” Ellie asked, moving over to stand in front of the cage. “Since when do you laugh, anyway?”

“Blame your grandfather,” a voice behind her said. Startled, Ellie spun around to see her grandmother sitting on the floor, leaning against the wall by the hallway to the study.

“Nonna, what happened? Are you okay?” Ellie rushed over to the old woman and crouched down next to her.

“I’m fine. I just stumbled and fell, and haven’t been able to find the energy to get myself up yet. Probably because I spent a good five minutes trying to hush that jungle chicken.”

“She was laughing because you fell?” she asked, horrified. Her grandmother looked mildly ashamed.

“No. I, er, may have let slip a curse word when I hit my hip on the way down. Back when she was younger, Marlowe picked up a few choice words from your grandfather and he thought it was the funniest thing, so he would laugh whenever she said them. Then *she* started laughing whenever *he*—or anyone else—cursed. The bird doesn't swear any more, thank heavens, but she still laughs like a maniac when she hears someone else do it."

"I've got to admit, that sounds like it would be pretty amusing," Ellie said with a chuckle. "Come on, let's get you up. Are you hurt?"

"I don't think so. Maybe a bit sore."

With her granddaughter's aid, the elderly woman made it to her feet. She put a hand on the wall for support and looked down at herself.

"Well, nothing's broken," she said. "Thanks for that, my dear. Sorry we woke you."

"Don't be sorry—you should have called out for me," Ellie admonished. "I'm here to help, you know."

She let her grandmother lean on her as they walked to the kitchen, then started making a pot of coffee, continuing to shoot surreptitious looks at the elderly woman while she ran the grinder. It struck her just how old her nonna was getting. She was at the age where a simple fall like that could be very serious. *What if I hadn't been here to help her?* Ellie wondered. *What if she falls again sometime while I'm at work, and breaks something?* The idea made her nervous, but she knew that her grandmother would brush off any attempts at a serious talk about her health. With a sigh, she set a mug of coffee down in front of her grandmother and grabbed the cream and sugar for her, as well as a silver spoon.

“I need to take Bunny outside,” she said. “But when we get in I want to run some ideas by you, okay?”

She shifted on her feet, watching the little dog nose her way through the dew-covered grass. It was a chilly morning, and she was wishing that she had worn something warmer than her sleeping clothes and bathrobe outside. The trees stood a few yards away, dark and looming, making her uncomfortable. *Anyone could be in there right now, watching me*, she thought with a shiver that had nothing to do with the cold. *I really hope that Sheriff Ward and his deputies catch Anthony's killer soon.* As she stared at the forest, which was part of a large state park, the thought came to her that Anthony Reeves' murder couldn't have been the first one that those trees had seen. A forest that old must have witnessed a whole host of crimes. She wondered how many people had gone missing in there, never to be found.

“You need to stop thinking like that, Eleanora Pacelli,” she said out loud. The shadows between the trees were beginning to look even more unfriendly than they had before. She was freaking herself out, which wouldn't lead to anything good. "Come on, Bunny. Let's go inside."

She turned to see her grandmother standing at the sliding porch door with the landline in her hand, and her face pale.

"It's for you," the elderly woman said when Ellie opened the door. "Come on, Bunny, let's go get you some breakfast and let your mom talk on the phone."

Ellie put the phone to her ear as her grandmother and the dog left the room. "Hello?"

"Ellie, it's me," Shannon's familiar voice said. She sounded hoarse, as if she were sick or had been crying. "I know it's really early, but I thought you should know… someone else has been killed. Another reporter. Someone I work with. Her name was Chloe. She was found just outside of town… on the side of the road. About two hours ago."

"Oh my goodness," she breathed, sitting down as what her friend was saying hit her. "I saw her yesterday. She stopped in at the pizzeria, trying to get me to do an interview with her. I'm so sorry, Shannon."

"I just can't believe that she's gone." Shannon took a deep breath. "I think my boss is going to try to set up a vigil for her tomorrow night. If she does, will you come? You might have been one of the last people to see her alive, and since you were also there when Anthony died… well, I think it would be fitting. Plus, I could use the support."

"Of course. Whatever you need. I'm here for you." Ellie looked out the window towards the woods, then squeezed her eyes shut. How many more people would die before the killer was caught?

CHAPTER THIRTEEN

Getting ready for the vigil was a somber affair. Ellie, who didn't have anything remotely appropriate in her own closet, put on a long black skirt of her grandmother's, along with the black blouse that she had worn to dinner at Shannon's just a couple of nights ago. Her hair was pulled up into a simple bun, and she kept her makeup to the bare minimum. When she walked downstairs, her grandmother gave her a once-over, wringing her hands.

"I wore that skirt to your grandfather's funeral," she said softly, half to herself. She cleared her throat. "It's a terrible thing, two deaths so close together. I can't imagine anyone taking one human life, let alone two. You be safe, all right, dear?"

"You, too," Ellie said, giving her grandmother a hug. "Lock the doors, and keep your cellphone handy in case you fall again. I know—you're fine. Just do it to humor me, okay? I don't want a repeat of yesterday."

She bent down to scratch Bunny behind the ears, said a quick goodbye to Marlowe, and then let herself out the door. She wasn't looking forward to the vigil, but putting it off wouldn't make her feel any better.

"Thanks for coming," Shannon said. "More people showed up than I expected."

"It is pretty busy," Ellie said, looking around the parking lot. Nearly every space was full, and the paths in the park were crowded.

In the center of the small park was a gazebo, which had been filled with electric candles and photos of both Chloe and Anthony. The two women headed toward the display, passing quiet people dressed in mournful colors. It was oddly quiet. Ellie couldn't remember the last time she had seen a crowd so silent. She was both amazed and touched at the turnout. Kittiport truly was a small, tightly knit community. She realized that most of these people had either known one or both of the deceased, or were friends with someone who did. Nearly everyone would have read Chloe's articles in the paper week after week. She didn't know what Anthony's job had been, but his family—his wife and two little girls—would be around here somewhere as well.

Does it make them feel better, she wondered, *seeing all of the people gathered here in support? Or does it make their grief come back in full force, seeing reminders of his death everywhere?* Her throat felt thick and sore, as if she were about to start crying. These two murders had been so senseless. She could only hope that the killer was done now, and no one else's picture would be put in the gazebo.

"I don't want to stay long," her friend said, sticking close to her side. "I just felt like I should come, since I was the last person to see Anthony alive, and I knew Chloe from work. I feel like it's somehow my fault. If only I hadn't been trying to dig up more information on that fish story."

"It's not your fault at all, Shannon," Ellie told the other woman. "There's only one person who's responsible for all of this—and that's the man that killed them. Blaming yourself won't help anything. Blame him."

Her friend was silent for a moment, then nodded. "You're right. Feeling sorry for myself won't help anything. I have to focus on what's important." A determined glint came into her eye.

"What are you thinking?" Ellie asked, feeling a prickling of concern.

"I'm thinking I need to do what's right. I need to do what Chloe and Anthony would have wanted. I need to go public with everything I know so far about the story."

"Are you sure that's a good idea?" she asked her friend, knowing that it was too late to change her mind. She recognized that determined look from their high school days. It couldn't hurt to try anyway, though. "I mean; you don't *know* that the killings were related to the bad fish from a few months ago. It's really just guessing and… and coincidence."

"I don't believe in coincidence," Shannon said. "Reporters would never get anywhere if they ignored obvious connections that were right in front of them."

"Okay, say you're right and Anthony and Chloe were both killed because they got too close to revealing who was responsible for the bad fish that killed that old man. Don't you think that he might set his sights on *you* next if you go public with everything?"

"I—" her friend faltered. "Maybe. You're right, he probably will. But James and Russell would protect me, don't you think? If the killer tries to come after me, he might even end up getting caught."

"Shannon, you're scaring me. If you have information that might help the investigation, then give it to Russell. In secret. Don't go public with it. It's not work the risk," Ellie said, stopping in her tracks and turning to face the other woman. "I mean it."

"You don't understand." Her friend took a deep breath. "I *want* to do this. This is what I wanted to be a journalist for. To give the public the truth. To find answers that no one else can. Not to… to report on the outcome of the latest quilting competition."

Ellie fell silent, staring at her friend, trying to judge how committed Shannon was to this insane idea. "Shannon… be careful, all right?" she said at last. "I don't want to see you getting hurt next."

"I will be," Shannon promised. "I don't want to join Anthony and Chloe in that gazebo. All I want is to stop the killings. Now, I'm sorry, but I've got to go and talk to my boss. If we hurry, we might be able to get the story in in time for the morning paper."

With that her friend was gone, disappearing into the crowd and leaving Ellie staring after her.

CHAPTER FOURTEEN

The little sleep that Ellie got that night was punctuated by increasingly frightening nightmares. Her anxiety for Shannon boiled over into her subconscious, leading to terrible dreams of finding her friend murdered or grievously injured. She woke up gasping a few times, and when she looked over at her clock was always surprised to find how little time had passed.

When at last the first rays of morning light came streaming in the window, Ellie nudged Bunny awake and sneaked down the stairs, careful not to wake the bird. She slipped into the kitchen to make a cup of coffee, then headed out onto the front porch with Bunny. She had no idea when the paper got delivered, but was determined not to miss it. She had to know if Shannon had actually gone through with it and had published whatever she had dug up on the case of the bad fish.

It was another chilly morning, but this time Ellie had brought an old wool blanket out with her. She wrapped it around her shoulders and sipped her steaming coffee as she stared out across the street at the ocean in the distance. It was grey right now, but once the sun came up higher she knew the waves would be dancing with reflected light. It was a beautiful view, but she couldn't take the time to enjoy it; instead, she looked anxiously up and down the street for the man who delivered the newspapers.

After what felt like ages she heard the puttering of an old car. She looked to her right and saw a vehicle coming from the direction of town. It paused at each house, and the driver tossed a newspaper in a thin plastic bag onto every driveway. Ellie stood up, holding Bunny in her arms. It seemed forever for the newspaper delivery man to reach her grandmother's house, but at last he pulled up to the end of the driveway and handed her the paper with a nod before driving to the next house. Anxious to read what was inside, Ellie went back indoors with her dog and sat at the kitchen table with her half-full cup of coffee to read the news.

When she saw the front page, her tight muscles unclenched. It was simply a story about the vigil the night before, asking for prayers for the families of the deceased and warning people to lock their doors and not go out at night, especially alone. She turned the page idly, believing that Shannon hadn't managed to get her story in on time. Her relief was cut short by what she saw on the second page.

It was a long paragraph, detailing the fish fiasco from a few months ago and the steps that the journalists at the *Kittiport Times* had taken to investigate it. The section ended with a warning.

It is believed that the recent murders of Anthony Reeves and Chloe McCullough may be related to the bad fish incident, which led to the death of an innocent man. If you have any information involving any of these three cases, please contact the sheriff's department directly.

The number to the department was listed, along with a headshot of Shannon. Ellie stared at the picture for a moment, nearly overwhelmed with fear for her friend. Then she took a deep breath and began to read the rest of the article. Shannon had published it in hopes that one of her readers might know something—anything—that could lead to the capture of the killer. The least she could do was read what her friend had written.

She skimmed through the first few sentences, which only covered what she already knew. A few months ago, a delivery of out-of-season fish had been made to a few different restaurants around town, including the White Pine Kitchen. An elderly man had eaten some and had passed away a few days later due to complications from food poisoning. Many other people around town had also gotten ill, though none as seriously as he had. The restaurants had been inspected, and it had been determined that none of them was at fault for mishandling the fish. After that, the investigation seemed to have stalled… or the official investigation, anyway.

Ellie scanned the article, looking for something useful. When she saw a business name that she recognized, she gasped. East Coast Delivery and Cold Storage had been the company that stored and transported the fish. *If something went wrong while they were storing it—a power outage or something—then that could mean the fish went bad on their watch,* she thought.

She got up and went to the study to get her laptop. Bringing it back to the kitchen table, she searched for the company online. Shannon had mentioned them for a reason. Did she think they had something to do with the bad fish… and the subsequent murders? Ellie knew that Clayton's uncle owned the company, but she didn't know much beyond that. Could his uncle be the killer?

She pulled up the company's website, and was both disappointed and relieved to see the picture of Clayton's uncle, Jedidiah Burke. He was a frail-looking elderly man, not at all what she had been picturing. There was no way he could have killed two people, *and* dragged a body through the forest and dumped it in the river.

Well, that's that, she thought. *Someone else must be the killer.* She looked through the article again, but Shannon hadn't mentioned anyone else by name. Ellie bit her lip, dissecting her own memories as she stared at the page. If the killer wasn't Jedidiah Burke, then who was it? Someone else related to the company, desperate to keep it from being shut down when their responsibility in the fish fiasco was exposed.

Ellie felt like a ball of ice had suddenly materialized in the pit of her stomach. Jedidiah might be too old to be committing any murders, but his nephew, Clayton, sure wasn't.

CHAPTER FIFTEEN

"Any luck?" Ellie asked, pressing her cellphone hard against her ear.

"No. He's not working today, and his cellphone is out of service range," the sheriff said from the other end. "We'll keep looking, but honestly, I'm not so sure it's him."

"It has to be," she said. "It all makes sense. If his uncle's cold storage units had some sort of malfunction, then they could be responsible for the fish going bad and the old man dying. Something like that, especially in a community this small, could put them out of business. Or get them sued. Killing to protect your job is good enough motive, isn't it?"

"I'm not saying I disagree with you, Ms. Pacelli. I did send Liam out to track the kid down, after all. But there are still a lot of unanswered questions. For example, how does Anthony Reeves fit in to all of this?"

"I don't know," Ellie said, sitting down in frustration. "Maybe he used to work for the Burkes. If so, he might have known that they were responsible for the fish going bad."

"*If* they're the ones responsible," Russell reminded her gently. She heard him sigh. "I'll look into it. Hold on a second, I should have his employment records on my computer still…"

She waited, tapping her fingernails on the table. It was well past noon. She had spent the last few hours anxiously waiting for updates, and had only recently given in and called the sheriff's department herself.

"Hmm," Sheriff Ward said at last. "It looks like Reeves's last known place of employment was at East Coast Delivery and Cold Storage. You may be on to something here. I'm going to head out and see if I can't find this Clayton kid myself."

"Wait," Ellie said before he hung up the phone. "Shannon… is she safe?"

"She's fine," he assured her. "For security reasons, I can't tell you where she is, but she's with James and an armed deputy. We're aware that she might be the killer's next target due to that article she wrote. We aren't going to let anything happen to her."

"Good," she breathed. "And good luck finding Clayton. I don't want him to have the chance to hurt anyone else."

Ellie waited. And waited. The hours passed by slowly, but still there was no call from Shannon, telling her that Clayton had been found. She managed to resist calling the sheriff's department again, knowing that Russell was already doing all he could to catch the murderer, but the not knowing was killing her. She had already called Jacob and Rose and let them know that she wouldn't be in to the pizzeria today—there was no way she would be able to concentrate. Instead she busied herself by tidying up around the house, always staying close to her cellphone so she wouldn't miss a call.

Gradually the afternoon wore on into evening, and Ellie still hadn't received news from anyone. She wondered if Clayton had read the article and fled, knowing that someone was bound to give his name to the police.

This isn't exactly how I wanted to spend my Thursday evening, she thought, leaning back in the chair at the desk in her grandfather's study. Thursday evening… why did that seem so important? Suddenly she sat up straight. Thursday evening! Clara and Clayton's date.

She picked up her phone with shaking fingers and dialed the sheriff's department. The receptionist told her that Sheriff Ward wasn't in, and Ellie ground her teeth in frustration.

"Can you put me through to his cellphone?" she asked. "It's important."

"Yes, just a second and I'll transfer you," the woman replied.

Ellie waited while the phone beeped and buzzed in her ear. Her heart leapt when it finally rang once, then sank again as a recorded message began to play, prompting her to leave a message. She quickly told Russell about the date, then hung up. Either his phone's battery was dead, or he was somewhere out of cell service—she was guessing the latter. There was no telling when he would hear it… and the date was in half an hour.

I need to warn Clara. She shouldn't be alone with Clayton, Ellie thought. She flipped through her phone's contacts, and sighed in annoyance when she realized that she didn't have Clara's number; it was pinned up in the pizzeria's kitchen just like all of the other employee's numbers.

"Clara has to know," she said at last, reluctantly accepting the knowledge that she was going to have to drive out to the White Pine Kitchen herself.

She tried calling the sheriff twice more on her way there, but got the same message both times. The little, logical voice in her head telling her that Clara probably wasn't in any danger was drowned out by the memories of all of the television shows and books she had read where innocent young women met their fates at the hands of cruel killers.

She parked her car right outside the restaurant and hurried in, barely pausing to notice the gorgeous entranceway or the soothing music that greeted her as she walked through the doors.

"Can I help you?" the host asked, remaining calm despite the fact that she had just burst in.

"I'm meeting someone," she gasped as she hurried past him, her eyes scanning the tables. She had to be somewhere… there. She spotted Clara and Clayton at a table near the back, just being served drinks.

She wove her way through the restaurant, stopping only when she drew near the table. Now if only she could draw Clara's attention without Clayton noticing her…

"Ms. Pacelli?" the young woman said, shocked. Clayton spun around in his seat and Ellie winced.

"Come with me, Clara. It's an emergency," she said.

"What are you talking about? Did something happen at the pizzeria?"

"No… it's nothing like that. Please, just trust me. Come here…"

Clara, confused, looked between her date and her boss. "Ms. Pacelli… I'm kind of busy here. What's going on?"

Ellie's breath hissed between her teeth. She watched Clayton warily, expecting him to make his move at any moment. She decided to throw caution to the wind. What was important right now was getting Clara out of there.

"He's the killer, Clara. We have to leave, it's not safe."

"What?" the young woman asked in a high-pitched voice. They were beginning to draw attention to themselves, which as far at Ellie was concerned, was just fine. The more witnesses there were, the less likely it was that the young man would try something.

"What are you talking about, Ms. P?" Clayton asked, looking back and forth between her and Clara. "Look, sit back down Clara, I didn't kill anyone."

"Yes you did. You did it to protect your uncle's business. The fish— "

"You think he killed that guy and the reporter lady?" Clara asked, hovering between sitting and standing, shooting a confused glance at Clayton.

"It all makes sense," Ellie said, trying to gather her thoughts. "Think about it, Clara. Anthony—the first person who got killed—used to work for the same delivery company that Clayton's uncle owns. He was trying to cover his tracks."

"Whoa, Anthony started working with us just a couple of weeks ago," Clayton said. "You're talking about that incident with the rotten fish that gave that old dude food poisoning, right? Tony didn't start at my uncle's company until after that. He got fired by his previous employer, some dude named Shawn, and my uncle decided to give him a chance."

"Besides, he couldn't have killed that reporter," Clara said, sounding more confident now. "She was killed Monday night, right? And found the next morning? Well, Clayton and I saw a movie, and I dropped him off at his apartment after since his car is in the shop. He doesn't even live in Kittiport, so there's no way he would have been able to get back to town and kill someone after I said goodbye to him."

Ellie opened her mouth to argue, but nothing came out. She felt heat rise in her cheeks as she began to realize her mistake. "I'm sorry, I… I just thought… Wait, did you say he went to work for someone named Shawn?"

Clayton nodded cautiously. Both he and Clara were looking at her like she had gone off the deep end.

"I'm so sorry, you two," she said. "I'll explain everything later. I've got to go."

CHAPTER SIXTEEN

Ellie hurried out to her car, ignoring the wary looks and hushed murmurs of the people she passed on her way out of the restaurant. The second she got into the driver's seat, she picked up her cellphone and tried calling Sheriff Ward again. It went to voicemail, so she left him another message, telling him to ignore her previous message and that she had a new idea about who the killer was.

After hanging up, she sat in her car in silence for a long moment, wondering what she was going to do. She needed to tell *somebody* what she had realized, but she had no idea where she could find the sheriff or his deputies. *No*, she realized, *that's not true. Russell told me where one of his deputies would be... guarding Shannon.* She put her car into gear and pulled out of the restaurant's parking lot. She didn't know where Shannon was, but Kittiport was a small town—there weren't that many places she could be. She decided to check her friend's house first, since it was on the way, and then stop at the sheriff's department on the off chance that they were there.

She pulled up to her friend's house, disappointed to see no sign of a police cruiser. *The sheriff must have them stashed somewhere else for protection,* she thought. *But where? The sheriff's department? Somewhere else completely?* She was just about to pull away when she noticed something odd. Both Shannon and James's cars were in the driveway. Was it possible that they were here, but the deputy had left? Ellie bit her lip, then decided to take the extra few seconds to go knock on the door and see. If they were there, she could at least tell Shannon that she suspected Shawn Franks and see if her suppositions matched the facts.

She left her car idling on the curb and walked across the grass to her friend's front door. She knocked, paused, then knocked again, listening for footsteps all the while. Just as she was about to give up and go to the sheriff's department, she heard someone approaching from the other side. The door opened, and she looked up expecting to see Shannon or her husband. Instead she saw the face of the very last person she wanted to run into—Shawn Franks.

He looked at her in surprise. "What are you doing here?"

"I'm, um, looking for Shannon. We were supposed to meet…" she lied, thinking quickly.

"She's not here. I'm, ah, housesitting. She had a family emergency out of town."

"Okay, I'll just go then—"

She was cut off by a scream from somewhere inside the house.

"Help! Someone help!" Shannon's voice was panicked, but recognizable.

Shawn and Ellie stared at each other for a moment, then they both moved at the same time: Ellie towards her car, and Shawn towards her. He was faster than she was, and pulled her roughly inside by her shoulder.

"You shouldn't have come here," he growled. "What happens next is your fault."

She heard the clunk of the deadbolt as he locked the door behind them. He shoved her forward, directing her down the hall and into the kitchen, where Shannon and James sat bound to chairs.

"Ellie!" Shannon exclaimed tearfully. "Oh my goodness, I'm so sorry, I didn't know it was you. I thought you were the police."

Shawn forced her into a chair next to her friend, then began rummaging around in the kitchen drawers.

"Don't you have any more tape here?" he grumbled. "I used all of the roll I brought on the two of you."

Shannon ignored him, her wide eyes still fixed on Ellie. James hadn't said anything; he seemed to be concentrating on trying to wriggle his hands out of the duct tape binding him to the chair.

"I don't understand," Elli whispered as the fisherman continued to search through the kitchen drawers in vein. "Russell said he sent one of his deputies to keep an eye on you."

"He did," Shannon replied just as quietly. "Bethany was here for most of the day, but she got an emergency call in from the department and had to go. Russell and Liam are out searching for the guy they thought was the killer, so she was the only one who could take the call. *He* showed up twenty minutes after she left."

Ellie looked back over at Shawn. He seemed distracted by his search for something to tie her up with. Would he even notice if she made a break for it? She could run and go get help for the others. *It's now or never*, she thought. *I won't be able to do anything once he finds some tape or a rope and ties me to this chair.* Deciding to take her chance while she could, Ellie jumped to her feet. She'd only taken a step towards the hallway before Shawn's head snapped around and his arm came up. He was pointing a gun at her.

"Run, and I shoot her," he said, shifting his aim to Shannon. "Try me. I dare you."

His voice was frighteningly calm. Shaking, Ellie slowly sat back down. He had already killed two people; she had no doubt that he would kill a third.

"I don't understand," she said. "Why are you doing this? Are you going to kill us all?"

"Just shut up," he said, pointing the gun at her again. "None of this is my fault, you hear? An idiot member of my crew left those fish sitting in the sun for hours. They didn't smell bad, and I wasn't going to take a loss of a few hundred dollars just because some worthless kid couldn't remember to do his job, so I sold the catch anyway and fired the guy responsible. Even if the fish *were* bad, I thought the restaurants would notice before they cooked them. I sure didn't think anyone would *die* from it."

"You killed Anthony because you knew he was going to talk," Shannon broke in. "And you killed Chloe because she was getting close. Now me… that article of mine must have really scared you, huh?"

Ellie usually appreciated her friend's attitude and desire for the truth, but now was most definitely not the time for it. She kicked the other woman under the table.

"Quit talking," Shawn snapped. "I mean it."

He kicked open the cupboard under the sink and bent down for a second, rising victoriously with a fresh roll of duct tape in his hand. Ellie quailed as he approached her. She was trapped. She didn't dare make a break for it; even if he didn't shoot her, he was sure to shoot Shannon and James. But if he managed to tie her up, then she would truly be helpless.

"Please, don't do this," she begged as he tore a long strip of duct tape off of the roll. He placed the gun on the table in easy reach, as a warning in case she tried anything, and reached for her wrist, which she jerked out of his grasp.

"Don't struggle, Ellie," James said in an oddly calm voice. "It will just make things worse."

Has he given up already? she thought, disappointed. She had expected more fight from the sheriff's brother. If he thought the situation was hopeless, then was there anything she could do?

Ellie felt the fight go out of her. Shawn reached for her wrist again, and this time she didn't resist as he taped it to the arm of the chair. He did the other one, then bent down to tape her ankles. That was when James made his move.

He lunged across the table, having managed to free one arm from the tape. His fingers closed around the gun that Shawn had been waving around, and in an instant his finger was on the trigger and the pistol was pointed at the fisherman's face. Shawn froze.

"Back up slowly," James said. "Keep your hands in the air where I can see them. You've killed two people and threatened my wife. I hope you believe me when I say I *will* shoot."

Shawn seemed to believe him, because he did what James said. Ellie began shaking again, this time with shock and relief.

"Ellie," James said, not taking his gaze off of the murderer. "The left arm of your chair is loose. You should be able to wiggle the dowel free pretty easily and get your hand loose. Once you do that, free yourself, then start working on Shannon. I'm going to keep my eyes on this guy until my brother gets here. You should NOT have messed with the Wards, Shawn Franks. We don't go down easily."

EPILOGUE

"Still having nightmares?" Ellie asked.

"Oh yeah," Shannon said. "I don't think they'll stop any time soon, either."

For someone who had been plagued by bad dreams for the past week since her near-death experience, the woman seemed oddly happy. Ellie suspected her friend's mood had something to do with why Shannon had wanted to meet for coffee in the middle of the day.

"Come on, spit it out," she said at last. "I know you're dying to tell me something. You always get a weird smile on your face when you're keeping a secret."

"I do not," her friend said, laughing. "But fine, since you insist. I just got news from my boss this morning. She wants me to start covering some of the bigger stories. She was impressed with how I handled this one."

"That's great news, Shannon," Ellie said. "This is huge for you. You should celebrate or something."

"Honestly, I kind of want to keep it quiet for now," Shannon said. "I mean, technically I'm taking Chloe's spot, which obviously I feel horrible about. I just needed to tell *someone* other than James. He didn't exactly have the reaction I was looking for."

Ellie raised her eyebrows. "I would have thought he would be proud of you. This is what you've wanted for years."

"He seems to think I'm going to stick my nose in the wrong story and get in trouble again," her friend said. She laughed. "I can't really blame him, I guess. Anyway, how have you been?"

"Not terrible, not great," Ellie said. "I'm glad that Shawn is behind bars, but I keep going over it all in my head, wondering how things got so out of control over some spoiled fish. People can be kind of horrible sometimes."

"Most people are good though," Shannon said. "It's just that the good is less noticeable than the bad most of the time. Oh, how is your grandmother? I should have asked about that first, I'm sorry."

"She's doing all right. Thank goodness she didn't break her hip the last time she fell. But that's three times in the last week and a half." Ellie bit her lip. "I'm worried about her, but I don't know what to do or how to bring it up. She's so determined to be independent."

"Isn't she having some family over in a couple of weeks? Maybe you could talk to them about it and stage some sort of intervention. Get her to use a walker or something," Shannon suggested.

"That's a good idea, but I'll have to wait and see how things go. This is my great-aunt and uncle and their son. If I ever met them before, I don't remember it. They may be family, but they're practically strangers," Ellie told her.

"Well, I'm sure you'll handle it just fine," her friend said. "You managed to survive this week, and I'm sure it was much worse than anything family could throw at you."

She has a point, Ellie thought, taking a sip of her coffee. *Compared to surviving these past few weeks, how bad can a visit from family be?*

Made in the USA
Lexington, KY
12 October 2016